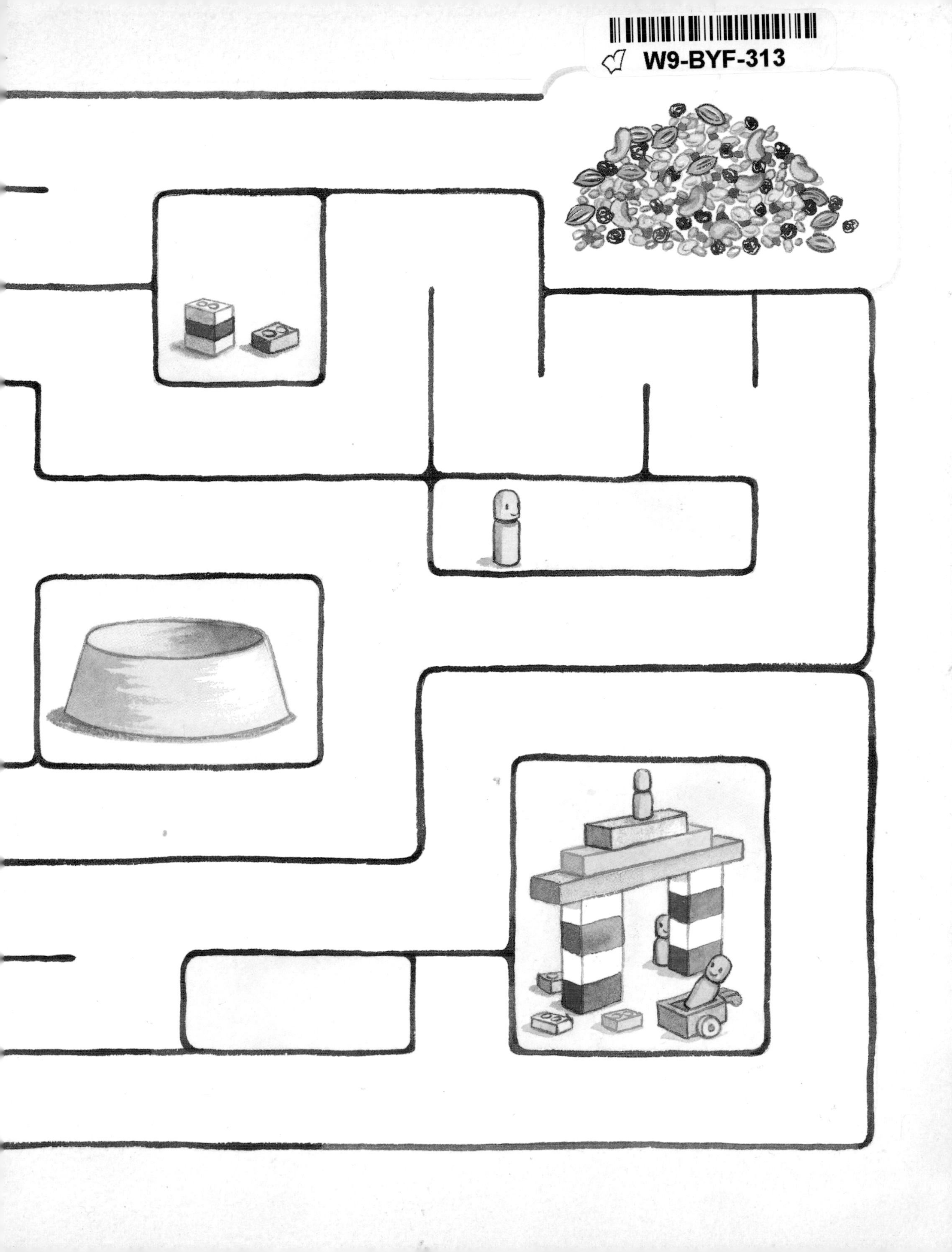

I Like to Read® books, created by award-winning picture book artists as well as talented newcomers, instill confidence and the joy of reading in new readers.

We want to hear every new reader say, "I like to read!"

Visit our website for flash cards, activities, and more about the series:
www.holidayhouse.com/ILiketoRead
#ILTR
This book has been tested by an educational expert and determined to be a guided reading level C.

For my mom, who always read to me

Printed and bound in April 2018 at Tien Wah Press, Johor Bahru, Johor, Malaysia.
The artwork was created with watercolors on Arches 90 lb. cold press paper.
www.holidayhouse.com
First Edition
1 3 5 7 9 10 8 6 4 2
Library of Congress Cataloging-in-Publication Data
Names: Schories, Pat, author, illustrator.
Title: Squeak the mouse likes his house / Pat Schories.
Description: First Edition. | New York : Holiday House, [2018] | Series: I like to read | Summary: "For a tiny mouse, a sneaker can be a bed and a few crumbs can be a meal"—Provided by publisher.
Identifiers: LCCN 2017043230| ISBN 9780823439430 (hardcover) | ISBN 9780823439447 (pbk.)
Subjects: | CYAC: Mice—Fiction. | Dwellings—Fiction.
Classification: LCC PZ7.S37645 Sq 2018 | DDC [E]—dc23 LC record available at https://lccn.loc.gov/2017043230

SQUEAK the Mouse
Likes His House

Pat Schories

HOLIDAY HOUSE • NEW YORK

Squeak the Mouse
likes his house.

Squeak the Mouse
likes the fun toys
at his house.

Squeak!

Squeak the Mouse
likes the cozy beds
at his house.

Squeak!

Squeak the Mouse
likes the fresh water
at his house.

Squeak!

Squeak the Mouse
likes the good books
at his house.

Squeak!

Squeak!
Squeak!

Squeak the Mouse
likes the free snacks
at his house.

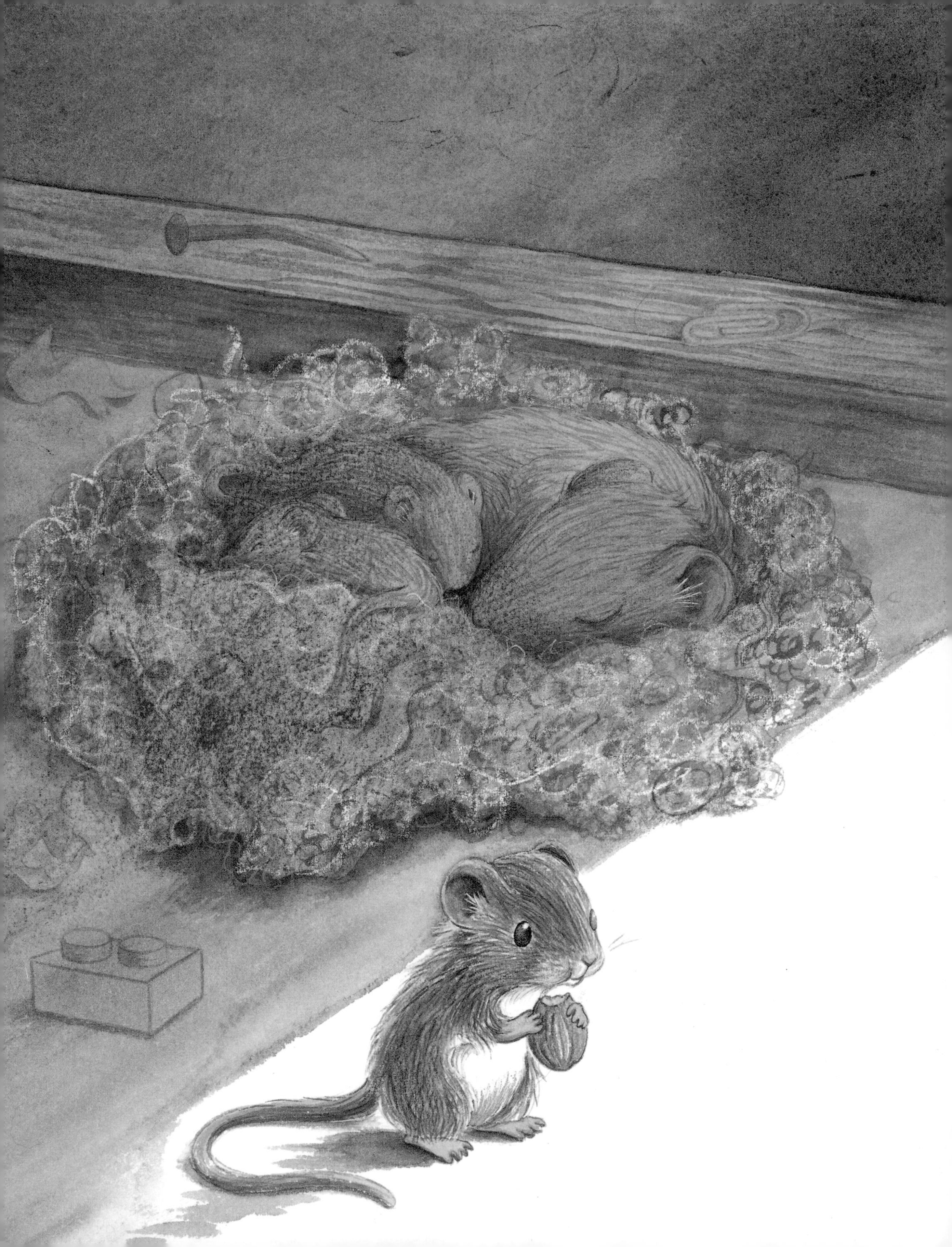

Squeak the Mouse
likes his house.
Squeak!

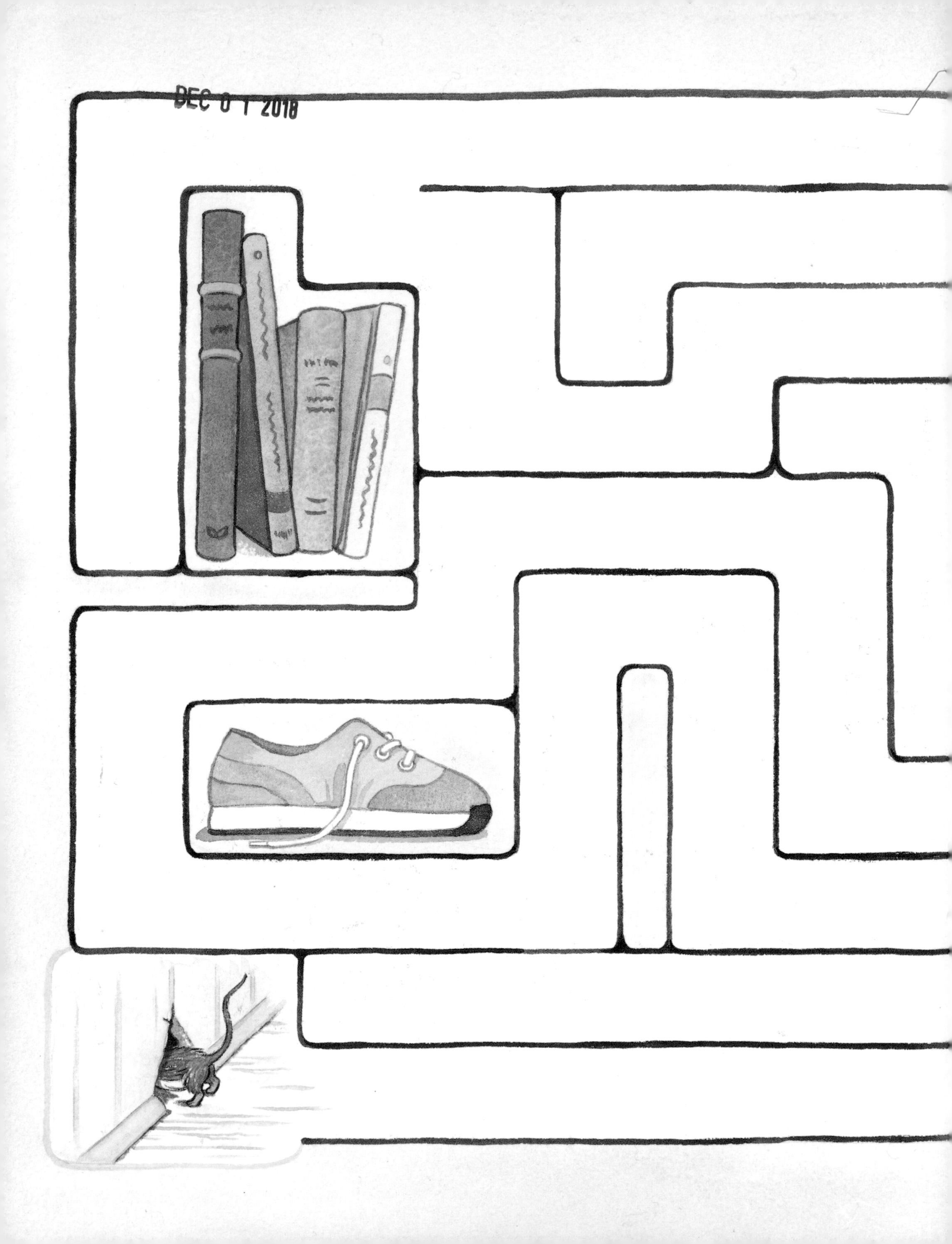